# LOONEY TUNES

# SYLVESTER & TWEETY

**READ THE MYSTERY**

# Granny Vanishes

Bath New York Singapore Hong Kong Cologne Delhi Melbourne

**Story by Sid Jacobson**
**Pencils by Pablo Zamboni and Walter Carzon**
**Inks by Duendes del Sur**
**Color by Barry Grossman**

First published by Parragon in 2008
Parragon
Queen Street House
4 Queen Street
Bath BA1 1HE, UK

ISBN 978-1-4075-2631-7

Printed in USA

Tweety, Sylvester, and Granny had traveled by train since early that morning.

"I'm so hungry," said Granny. "I could eat a delicious salad."

Tweety heard his tiny stomach growl. "And I could eat a dewicious bunch of birdseed," he thought.

"And I could eat **YOU**, you delicious-looking canary,"
Sylvester's eyes seemed to say to Tweety.

"Why don't you boys find us seats in the dining car,"
Granny told her two pets. She reached into the pocket of her
new coat, which was hung up behind her, for a hankerchief.

"I'll be right along," she added, waving them out the door.
"And remember, no funny business, Sylvester. Or I'll send
you home at the next station."

This was a special trip for Granny. She was traveling far across Europe to see her twin sister, Harriet, for the first time since they were small. They had written letters, of course, and had even spoken on the phone. Granny wondered if they would still look alike.

Meanwhile, Sylvester chased Tweety all the way to the dining car, screaming that he was going to eat him.
"Gwanny is going to send you home!" Tweety warned him.

That threat finally stopped Sylvester's mean behavior.

They soon arrived at the dining car and were given a table at the window. You could see that the cat was still ready to spring at Tweety, but he was too afraid of being sent home. So they sat and waited. And waited. And waited . . .

The dining car soon filled up, but there was no sign of Granny. "Where could she be?" Tweety asked, sadly. Even Sylvester was worried. Could Granny be sick? Had she seen him taunt Tweety? Gulp, could she have found a nicer cat? The two pets raced back toward Granny's stateroom.

What they found there was even more mysterious.
Granny had disappeared! Then Tweety saw it. Written into the
dust on the state room's window was the word "HELP!"
It was the message Granny had left behind.

"Wh-wh-what does this m-mean?" stammered the trembling cat.

"I'm not sure," answered Tweety, "but we're going to solve this myste-wy. Gwanny is in twouble!"

They hunted up and down the aisle of the train, opening every door. They scampered into closets, looked under tables and chairs and benches and found . . . NOTHING! Granny was gone. The train came to a stop at the next station.

"Look!" Tweety shrieked, gazing out the window.

Two men had just walked off the train. One was pushing the other away from the train car. He was a fat man with a pudgy, angry face. The man being held was wearing a hat and he had a long beard. He also wore a very familiar coat.

"That's Gwanny's new coat!" said Tweety. "That must be Gwanny in the beard!"

"Hurry, puddy tat," Tweety called out. "We must follow Gwanny!"
They jumped off the train and raced after the two men.

The men headed for a car parked in a lot behind the station. Tweety and Sylvester trailed them, unseen.

"I recognized you the moment I saw you!" the fat man growled. "At last, the great master spy is in the hands of Herman Vermin!"

The fat man and the bearded person got inside the car. The two pets scurried through an open window and hid in the car. The bearded person had tape over his—or her—mouth and couldn't speak.

"He's Herman Vermin," whispered Sylvester, "but is that Granny?"

Herman Vermin ripped off the fake beard from the other's face.

"I knew it," laughed Herman. "It's you, MOTHER HARRIET!"

"Mother Harriet?" groaned Sylvester. "It's not Granny. We followed the wrong person!"

"Of course, it's Gwanny," said Tweety. "Herman has mistaken her for Gwanny's twin sister Hawiet!"

"We've got to save Gwanny," he whispered to the cat.
"We've got to save her in any way we can! And we've
got to act vewy fast!"

"Yes," Herman was saying, "I've captured the master spy after all these years."

The tape over Granny's mouth stopped her from saying anything. So, Tweety flew up off the floor and went into action.

"What is this?!" Herman screamed, as the canary flapped his
wings in the man's face. "A secret weapon?"
 Sylvester leaped out from the back and jumped for Herman's leg.
"Ouch!" Herman screamed. "They're attacking me from all sides!"

Tweety removed the key in the ignition lock and, holding it in his mouth, he flew out of the front window of the car.

"The car key!" Herman shrieked. "I can't move the car without it!" Then he raced after the fleeing Tweety.

Hearing the noise, police quickly came and rescued Granny. They then arrested Herman Vermin for kidnapping—that is, GRANNY-napping.

With tears in her eyes, Granny thanked her two pets, as they all headed for the train station.

This time they were headed in the **OPPOSITE** direction, away
from Granny's sister, who was now the famous spy, Mother Harriet!
"I guess I can wait another fifty years to see my sister again,"
Granny smiled. "I've done pretty well with just the two of you!"